CANARY
COTTAGE

MOLE'S
HOUSE

S

RAT'S
HOUSE

OSIER
BED

OTTER'S
HOUSE

PAN
ISLAND

THE
WEIR

THE RETURN
of
THE HERO

KENNETH GRAHAME

Illustrated by Ernest H. Shepard

Aladdin Books
Macmillan Publishing Company
New York

Maxwell Macmillan International Publishing Group
New York   Oxford   Singapore   Sydney

First Aladdin Books edition 1991

The Wind in the Willows originally published 1908 by Charles Scribner's Sons
Text copyright © 1991 Methuen Children's Books
This presentation copyright © 1991 Methuen Children's Books
Line illustrations copyright © 1933 Charles Scribner's Sons, renewal
copyright © 1961 E. H. Shepard. Coloring-in copyright © 1970, 1971
by E. H. Shepard and Methuen Children's Books Ltd.

Aladdin Books
Macmillan Publishing Company
866 Third Avenue
New York, NY 10022

The Return of the Hero first published in this format 1991
by Methuen Children's Books.

Printed in Hong Kong by Wing King Tong

1   2   3   4   5   6   7   8   9   10

Library of Congress CIP data is available

ISBN 0-689-71497-1

THE RETURN
OF THE HERO

Toad, flung into prison for stealing a motor-car, has escaped, disguised as a washerwoman. Still far from home, he has spent the night in a strange wood.

Toad awoke early and, sitting up, wondered for a moment where he was. Then he remembered – he was free!

He marched forth into the morning sun, wondering which way to go. With police scouring the country for him to drag him off to prison again, every minute was of importance. Presently, round a bend in the canal, a solitary horse came plodding with a long line attached to his collar.

With a swirl of water, the barge he was drawing slid up, its occupant a big stout woman, one brawny arm laid on the tiller.

"Nice morning, ma'am!" she remarked.

"I dare say, ma'am!" responded Toad, "to them that's not in trouble like what I am. My daughter sends off to me to come at once; so, fearing the worst, I left my business to look after itself—I'm in the washing and laundering line, ma'am—and now I've lost my money, and lost my way."

"Where might your daughter be living, ma'am?" asked the barge-woman.

"Close to a fine house called Toad Hall," replied Toad. "You may have heard of it."

"Why, I'm going that way myself,"
replied the woman. "I'll give you a lift."

Toad stepped lightly on board. Toad's
luck again! he thought.

"So you're in the washing business,
ma'am?" said the barge-woman politely.
"Are you *very* fond of washing?"

"I love it," said Toad. "I simply dote on
it. Never so happy as when I've got both
arms in the wash-tub!"

"What a bit of luck, meeting you!"
observed the barge-woman thoughtfully.

"Why?" asked Toad nervously.

"Well," replied the woman. "My
husband's such a fellow for shirking his
work and leaving the barge to me—how
am I to get on with my washing? There's
a heap of things in the cabin. If you'll take
one or two and put them through the
wash-tub, it'll be a pleasure to you, as you
rightly say, and a real help to me."

"Here, you let me steer!" said Toad, now thoroughly frightened. "I might spoil things, or not do 'em as you like."

"Let you steer?" replied the woman, laughing. "It takes practice to steer properly. Besides, it's dull, and I want you to be happy. You do the washing."

Toad resigned himself to his fate. I suppose any fool can *wash*! he thought. He selected a few garments and set to.

A long half-hour passed, and every minute saw Toad getting crosser. His back ached and he noticed with dismay that his paws were getting all crinkly.

He muttered words that should never pass the lips of washerwomen or Toads and lost the soap, for the fiftieth time.

A burst of laughter made him look round. The woman was laughing till tears ran down her cheeks. "I thought you were an imposter all along," she gasped.

Toad's temper boiled over. "You common, low, *fat* barge-woman!" he shouted; "I would have you know that I am a very well known, respected, distinguished Toad!"

The barge-woman peered under his bonnet. "So you are!" she cried. "A nasty, crawly Toad in my nice clean barge! Now that I will *not* have."

One big mottled arm shot out and caught Toad by a fore-leg, while the other gripped him by a hind-leg. Then the world turned upside down and Toad found himself flying through the air. He reached the water with a loud splash.

He rose to the surface spluttering and saw the barge-woman laughing.

He struck out for the shore and started to run after the barge. He unfastened the tow-rope, jumped lightly on the horse's back and urged it to a gallop. Looking back, he saw that the barge had run aground and the barge-woman was shouting, "Stop, stop!" Toad, laughing, spurred his steed onward.

Toad had travelled some miles when he found he was on a wide common. Near him stood a gypsy caravan beside which a man was sitting, staring into the wide world. Near by, over a fire, hung an iron pot and out of that pot came forth rich and varied smells. Toad now knew that he had not been really hungry before. This was the real thing at last, and no mistake. He looked the gypsy over, and the gypsy looked at him.

Presently the gypsy remarked, "Want to sell that there horse of yours?"

It had not occurred to Toad to turn the horse into cash, but he badly wanted ready money and a solid breakfast.

"What?" he said, "me sell this beautiful young horse of mine? O no; it's out of the question. This horse is a cut above you altogether. All the same, how much might you be disposed to offer me?"

The gypsy looked the horse over. "Shillin' a leg," he said briefly.

"A shilling a leg?" cried Toad. "O no; I could not think of accepting four shillings for this beautiful young horse."

"Well," said the gypsy, "I'll make it five shillings, and that's my last word."

Toad pondered. At last he said, "Look here! You hand over six shillings and sixpence, and as much breakfast as I can possibly eat. In return, I will turn over to you my spirited young horse, with the beautiful harness thrown in."

The gypsy grumbled frightfully, but he counted out six shillings and sixpence. Then he tilted the pot, and a glorious stream of hot stew gurgled into a plate. Toad stuffed, and stuffed, and stuffed.

When he had taken as much stew as he could possibly hold, he set forth again in the best possible spirits.

As he tramped along, he thought of his adventures, and his pride began to swell within him. "Ho, ho!" he said to himself, "what a clever Toad I am!" But his pride was shortly to have a severe fall.

After some miles he reached the high road and, as he glanced along its white length, he saw approaching him something very familiar; a double note of warning fell on his delighted ear.

"This is more like it!" said the excited Toad.

He stepped out confidently into the road to hail the motor-car. Suddenly he became very pale, his knees shook and he collapsed. The approaching car was the very one he had stolen that fatal day when all his troubles began!

He sank down in a miserable heap in the road, murmuring, "It's all over now! Prison again! O, hapless Toad!"

The terrible motor-car drew slowly nearer till at last he heard it stop just short of him. Two gentlemen got out and one of them said, "O dear! Here is a poor washerwoman who has fainted in the road! Let us take her to the village, where doubtless she has friends."

They tenderly lifted Toad into the motor-car and proceeded on their way.

When Toad heard them talk in so kind a manner, and knew that he was not recognized, his courage began to revive.

"Look!" said one of the gentlemen. "The fresh air is doing her good. How do you feel now, ma'am?"

"A great deal better, thank you, sir," said Toad in a feeble voice. "I was only thinking, if I might sit on the front seat, where I could get the fresh air full in my face, I should soon be all right again."

"What a sensible woman!" said the gentleman. "Of course you shall."

Toad was almost himself again by now.

He looked about him and the old cravings rose up and took possession of him entirely. He turned to the driver at his side.

"Please, sir," he said, "would you let me try and drive the car for a little. It looks so easy and I should like to be able to tell my friends I had driven!"

The driver laughed and the gentleman said, "Bravo, ma'am! I like your spirit. Let her have a try."

Toad eagerly took the wheel, listened with affected humility to the instructions given him, and set the car in motion.

The gentlemen clapped their hands, saying, "Fancy a washerwoman driving as well as that, the first time!"

Toad went faster; then faster still.

He heard the gentlemen call out, "Be careful, washerwoman!" This annoyed him and he began to lose his head.

"Washerwoman, indeed!" he shouted recklessly. "I am Toad, the motor-car snatcher, the prison-breaker, the Toad who always escapes!"

With a cry of horror they rose and flung themselves on him. "Seize him!" they cried. "Bind him, chain him!"

Alas! they should have thought to stop the motor-car first. With a turn of the wheel Toad sent the car crashing into the thick mud of a horse-pond.

Toad landed with a thump, picked himself up and set off, running till he was breathless and had to settle down into a walk. When he had recovered somewhat, he began to giggle.

"Ho! ho!" he cried. "Toad comes out on top! Clever Toad! O, how very clev—"

A noise behind him made him turn his head. O misery! O despair! A chauffeur and two policemen were running towards him! Poor Toad pelted away again. He ran desperately, but they still gained steadily.

He struggled on wildly when suddenly splash! he found himself head over ears in deep, rapid water. In his panic he had run straight into the river!

He tried to grasp the reeds that grew along the water's edge, but the stream was so strong that it tore them out of his hands. He saw he was approaching a big dark hole in the bank, and as the stream bore him past he caught hold of the edge. As he stared into the hole, something twinkled in its depths—a familiar face. It was the Water Rat!

The Rat put out a paw, gripped Toad by the scruff of the neck and gave a great pull. The water-logged Toad came up slowly but surely. At last he stood in the hall, streaked with mud and weeds, but happy and high-spirited as of old.

"O, Ratty!" he cried. "I've been through such times since I saw you last! Such trials and sufferings, all so nobly borne! Such escapes, such disguises. O, I *am* a smart Toad, and no mistake!"

"Toad," said the Water Rat, firmly, "go upstairs at once, take off that old cotton rag and clean yourself, put on some of my clothes and try and come down looking like a gentleman if you *can*; for a more shabby, bedraggled object than you are I never set eyes on! Now, stop swaggering and arguing, and be off!"

By the time Toad came down again luncheon was on the table.

While they ate, Toad told the Rat all
his adventures, dwelling chiefly on his
own cleverness and cunning.

At last the Rat said, "Toady, don't you
see what an awful ass you've been making
of yourself? On your own admission you
have been imprisoned, chased, insulted,
jeered at and flung in the water! All
because you must go and steal a motor-
car. When are you going to be sensible
and try to be a credit to your friends?"

Toad heaved a deep sigh and said very humbly, "Quite right, Ratty! I've been a conceited old ass, but now I'm going to be good. We'll have our coffee, and then I'm going to stroll down to Toad Hall. I've had enough adventures."

"Stroll down to Toad Hall?" cried the Rat. "You mean you haven't heard about the Stoats and Weasels?"

"The Wild Wooders?" cried Toad, trembling. "What have they been doing?"

"—and how they've taken over Toad Hall?" continued the Rat.

Toad leaned his chin on his paws; and a tear welled up in each of his eyes, and splashed on the table, plop! plop!

"Go on," he murmured; "tell me all."

"When you got into trouble," said the Rat, "it was a good deal talked about. The Riverbankers stuck up for you, but the Wild Wood animals got very cocky, and went about saying you would never come back again! But Mole and Badger stuck out, through thick and thin that you would come back again somehow. They arranged to move into Toad Hall, and have it all ready for you when you turned up. They didn't guess what was going to happen, of course.

"One dark night a band of weasels, armed to the teeth, crept up to the front entrance; a body of desperate ferrets possessed themselves of the back-yard, and a company of skirmishing stoats occupied the conservatory.

"Mole and Badger were sitting by the fire, suspecting nothing, when those villains rushed in from every side. They beat them with sticks and turned them out into the cold and wet! And the Wild Wooders have been living in Toad Hall ever since, eating, drinking, singing vulgar songs—and telling everybody that they've come to stay for good."

"O, have they!" said Toad, seizing a stick. "I'll jolly soon see about that!"

"It's no good, Toad!" called the Rat after him. "You'll only get into trouble."

But there was no holding him. He marched down the road, his stick over his shoulder, till he got near his front gate. Suddenly there popped up a long yellow ferret with a gun.

"Who comes there?" said the ferret.

"Stuff and nonsense!" said Toad angrily.

The ferret raised his gun.

Toad dropped flat, and *Bang!* a bullet whistled over his head. As Toad scampered off down the road he heard the ferret laughing.

"What did I tell you?" said the Rat. "They are all armed. You must just wait."

Still, Toad was not inclined to give in at once. So he got out the boat, and set off up the river to where the garden of Toad Hall came down to the waterside.

All seemed very peaceful and deserted. Very warily he paddled up to the mouth of the creek, and was just passing under the bridge, when . . . *Crash!* A great stone smashed through the bottom of the boat. It filled and sank, and Toad found himself struggling in deep water. Looking up, he saw two stoats leaning over the bridge, watching him with glee.

The indignant Toad swam to shore, while the stoats laughed and laughed.

Toad retraced his weary way on foot.

"*What* did I tell you?" said the Rat crossly. "And look! You've lost my boat and ruined that nice suit that I lent you! Now sit down and have your supper, and be patient. We can do nothing until we have seen the Mole and the Badger, and heard their latest news. Those poor animals have been camping out, keeping a constant eye on the stoats and weasels, and planning how to get your property back for you. You don't deserve to have such loyal friends, Toad, you don't really."

They had just finished their meal when there came a knock at the door and in walked Mr Badger, looking very rough and tousled and the Mole, very shabby and unwashed.

"Here's Toad!" cried the Mole. "You managed to escape, you clever Toad!"

"Don't egg him on, Mole!" said the Rat, "but please tell us what the position is."

"The position's about as bad as it can be," replied the Mole grumpily.

"It's useless to think of attacking," said the Badger. "They're too strong."

"Then it's all over," sobbed Toad. "I shall never see my Toad Hall anymore!"

"Cheer up!" said the Badger. "I'm going to tell you a great secret: there is an underground passage, that leads from the river bank right up into Toad Hall."

"O, nonsense! Badger," said Toad.

"Your father showed it to me," said Badger severely. "'Don't let my son know about it,' he said. 'He's a good boy, but simply cannot hold his tongue.' Now, there's going to be a big banquet tomorrow. All the weasels will be in the dining-hall, eating and drinking and suspecting nothing.

"No guns, no swords, no arms whatever! They will trust entirely to their excellent sentinels. Now, that tunnel leads right up under the pantry, next to the dining-hall!"

"We shall creep out into the pantry," cried the Mole, "and rush in on them—"

"—and whack 'em, and whack 'em, and whack 'em!" cried the Toad in ecstasy.

"Very well," said the Badger, "our plan is settled. We will make all the necessary arrangements tomorrow morning."

When Toad got down next morning he found Badger reading the paper and Rat running round the room, distributing weapons in four little heaps on the floor.

Presently the Mole came tumbling in, very pleased with himself. "I've been getting a rise out of the stoats!" he said. "I put on Toad's old washerwoman dress, and off I went to Toad Hall. The sentries were on the look-out, of course, with their guns. The sergeant in charge said, 'Run away, my good woman!' 'Run away?' says I; 'it won't be me that'll be running away, in a short time from now! A hundred bloodthirsty Badgers are going to attack Toad Hall this very night,' said I. 'Six boat-loads of Rats will come up the river, while a battalion of Toads will storm the orchard. There won't be much left of you unless you clear out while you have the chance.'

"They were all as flustered as could be, saying, 'That's *just* like the weasels. They have fun while we are cut to pieces by bloodthirsty Badgers.'"

"*Moly,* how could you?" said the Rat.

"You've spoiled everything!" cried Toad.

"Mole," said the Badger, "I see you have more sense in your little finger than some have in the whole of their fat bodies. Good Mole! Clever Mole!"

Toad couldn't make out what Mole had done that was so clever.

When it began to grow dark, the Rat
proceeded to dress them up for the
expedition. There was a belt, a sword, a
cutlass, pistols, a truncheon, handcuffs,
bandages and a lunch box.

The Badger laughed and said, "All
right, Ratty! But I'm going to do all I've
got to do with this here stick."

But the Rat only said, *"Please,* Badger!
I shouldn't like you to say I had forgotten
anything!"

Badger led them along the river for a little way, then suddenly swung himself over the edge into a hole in the river bank: they were in the secret passage!

It was cold, and dark, and damp, and low, and narrow. They shuffled along, till at last they heard, apparently over their heads, people shouting and cheering and stamping on the floor.

"*What* a time they're having!" said the Badger. "Come on!" They hurried along the passage till they found themselves under a trap-door. They heaved it back, and found themselves standing in the pantry, with only a door between them and their enemies.

The noise was deafening. A voice could be made out saying, "I should like to say one word about our kind host, Mr Toad." (great laughter) — "*Good* Toad, *modest* Toad!" (shrieks of merriment).

Badger took a firm grip of his stick, cried, "The hour is come! Follow me!"— and flung the door wide open.

My!

What a squealing and a squeaking and a screeching filled the air!

Mighty Badger; Mole, black and grim; Rat, desperate and determined; Toad, frenzied with excitement, emitting Toad-whoops that chilled them to the marrow! They were but four in all, but to the panicstricken weasels the hall seemed full of monstrous animals, whooping and flourishing enormous clubs; and they fled with squeals of terror, through the windows, up the chimney, anywhere to get out of reach of those terrible sticks.

Up and down the hall strode the four friends, whacking with their sticks at every head that showed itself.

In five minutes the room was cleared.

"Mole," said the Badger, "you're the best of fellows! Just cut along outside and see what those stoat-sentries of yours are doing."

The Mole vanished promptly through a window. The Badger bade the other two see if they could find materials for a supper. "I want some grub," he said.

They were just about to sit down when the Mole clambered through the window, chuckling, with an armful of rifles.

"It's all over," he reported. "As soon as the stoats, who were very jumpy already, heard the uproar inside the hall, they threw down their rifles and fled. So *that's* all right!"

They finished their supper in great joy and contentment, and retired to rest, safe in Toad's ancestral home, won back by matchless valor and a proper handling of sticks.

The following morning the Badger
remarked: "I'm sorry, Toad, but there's a
heavy morning's work in front of you.
You see, we really ought to have a
banquet to celebrate this affair. It's
expected of you. Invitations have to be
written, and you've got to write 'em."

"What!" cried Toad, dismayed. "On a
jolly morning like this! Certainly not! I'll
be—Stop a minute, though! Why, of
course, dear Badger! It shall be done."

Toad hurried to the writing-table. A
fine idea had occurred to him.

He *would* write the invitations; and he would give a program of entertainment for the evening with speeches and songs by Toad! The idea pleased him mightily and he worked very hard and got all the letters finished by noon. A small weasel hurried off to deliver them.

But when the other animals came back to luncheon, the Rat caught Toad by the arm. "Now, look here, Toad!" he said. "It's about this banquet. I am very sorry, but there are going to be no speeches and no songs."

Toad's pleasant dream was shattered.

"Mayn't I sing them just one *little* song?" he pleaded piteously.

"No, not *one*," replied the Rat firmly, though his heart bled. "It's for your own good, Toady; you know your songs and speeches are all boasting and vanity; you *must* turn over a new leaf."

Toad remained a long while plunged in thought. At last he said in broken accents, "You have conquered, my friends. It was a small thing that I asked. However, you are right, I know. But, O dear, this is a hard world!"

He left the room with faltering steps.

"I feel like a brute," said the Rat.

"I know," said the Badger. "But would you have him jeered at by weasels?"

"Of course not," said the Rat. "And I came upon that weasel and confiscated Toad's invitations. They were disgraceful. Mole is filling out plain invitation cards."

The hour for the banquet drew near and Toad, still melancholy, pondered deeply. Gradually he began to smile. Then he took to giggling. He got up, locked the door, drew the curtains and, swelling visibly, sang: *"Toad's last little song!"*

The Toad—came—home!
There was panic in the parlor
   and howling in the hall,
There was crying in the cow-shed
   and shrieking in the stall,
When the Toad—came—home!

Shout—Hooray!
And let each one of the crowd
   try and shout it very loud,
In honor of an animal of
   whom you're justly proud,
For it's Toad's—great—day!

He sang this very loud, with great feeling. Then he heaved a deep sigh and went quietly down to his guests.

The animals cheered when he entered, and crowded round to say nice things about his courage and his fighting; but Toad only smiled faintly and murmured, "Not at all!" or, "On the contrary!"

When, later, there were cries of "Toad! Speech! Song!" Toad only shook his head and raised a paw in mild protest.

He was indeed an altered Toad!

After this, the four animals continued to lead their lives in great contentment. Sometimes they would stroll in the Wild Wood, now tamed, and it was pleasing to hear mother-weasels say, "Look, baby! There's the great Mr Toad! And that's the gallant Water Rat, with the famous Mr Mole and the terrible gray Badger!"